TAPESTRY

TAPESTRY

A Medieval Tale of Curses, Crowns, and Courage

Jerry Smith

ISBN: 978-1-64826-504-4   (Paperback Edition)
ISBN: 978-1-64826-508-2   (Hardcover Edition)
ISBN: 978-1-64826-495-5   (E-book Edition)

Some characters and events in this book are fictitious. Any similarity to real persons, living or dead, is coincidental and not intended by the author.

Book Ordering Information

Phone Number: 347-901-4929 or 347-901-4920
Email: info@globalsummithouse.com
Global Summit House
www.globalsummithouse.com

Printed in the United States of America

Contents

Preface vii

The Knight 1

The Mage.. 3

The Princess.. 5

The Young Man 6

Black Army 9

Knight's Final Ride 11

Princess's Plight 13

The King 15

Amidst The Chaos 17

Encounter In The Forest 18

   The Silver Dragon 19

Night Has Fallen 21

   Enter Sorceress 21

Battle At King's Castle 23

Journey West 24

Fall Of King's Castle 26

Friend Or Foe 27

Before The Fall 29

Ambush 30

The Final Battle 32

Happily Ever After...? 36

Preface

Once upon a time lost and now so very old
    Brave men became noble knights that were very bold
When the lands were ruled by just and peaceful great kings
    Bards would tell tales and with music they would doth sing
Of beautiful maidens and great deeds of brave knights
    Underneath clear, moonlit, warm, star-filled summer nights
Where swords and sorcery clashed 'tween evil and good
    Great monuments were built where brave heroes once stood
Dragons and other creatures would roam wild and free
    Amidst the vast forests filled with majestic trees
The seasons would come and then quickly come to pass
    Which now brings us to a wonderous tale at last.... .

The Knight

A chivalrous knight in armor of midnight black
    Mounts firmly upon his trusted steed's sturdy back
This beautiful horse all in alabaster white
    Together they forge out into the cold dark night
As the portcullis of the castle lifts away
    The two companions move forward along their way
Across the drawbridge upon their most noble quest
    Into this cruel unforgiving night without rest
Out into this turbulent vast world across land
10   Righting wrongs and unjust, taking a stoic stand
Heroic knight with his big fragile heart of gold
    Bearing forth with his ideals born from thee, now old
So much in this new world is changed and now gone past
    Burden of the quest is his to carry at last
Winds begin to blow and heavy snow starts to fall
    Noble knight pushes forward to answer his call

The trials of this journey have now just begun
    'Tis a long way off 'til the rise of the day's sun
Onward through this winter's night storm for they must go
20   Along the righteous path amidst the mounting snow
Laboriously down heavy snow covered trail
    The companions of good continue without fail
Trudging along the blanketed white covered fields
    Conviction within their souls won't waver or yield
As the castle completely fades in the distance
    Battling against the storm with much resistance
Suddenly, a massive silver dragon appears
    Gallantly, knight and steed stand firm despite their fears
Drawing forth his sword of truth, they begin their charge

30   Attacking the enormous dragon, looming large
    Slashes strike 'pon the foes in a blink of their eyes
        Upon the fallen snow, this brave hero now lies
    As the blood stains the ground from a wound to his head
        This brave knight will not be left behind to the dead

    Dragon defeated, the battle is now over
        The wounds to the knight continue to spill over
    Weary and injured the knight struggles to move on
        As the sun rises to signal the break of dawn
    Gazing 'round, the knight's steed is nowhere to be seen
40   Asking the heavens for help and to intervene
    Searching deep within, down into his very soul
        Discovering the strength to make himself now whole
    Slight movement catches his eye, something in the brush
        Cautiously approaching, preparing for a rush
    Knight's calm blue eyes scanning the brush for his quarry
        Injured, weary, ready to fight in full glory
    A flash of blinding light and the world starts to fade
        Down into the snow, this hero is gently laid

The Mage

Cloaked in robes of grey, looking up from ancient page
50 Stands before an altar, a sinister cruel mage
Driven upon the utter destruction of man
  Culminating the details of his master plan
Evil runs deep through his cold blood and onyx heart
  Rage boils within him to tear this good land apart
Devoted acolyte bows down on bended knees
  Looking up into the darkness is all he sees
A fierce fire burns within the mage's cold black eyes
  The acolyte screams, convulses, lays down and dies
"That brave knight of light cannot be allowed to live!"
60 All of his evil power to this, he must give
Ascending the steep stone steps into his noir keep
  Silent as death, the grey mage continues to creep
A special item is needed in that tower
  An ancient crystal that will unlock great power

Opening the door to the ancient room so old
  Where no other would go, not even men so bold
Removing the locks upon the old wooden chest
  Grasping the blood red crystal from where it should rest
A strange glow and pulse emanates within his hand
70 A terrible force to unleash upon this land
Upon the parapet, the grey mage faces east
  Preparing to bring forth such a terrible beast
As light lifts night by the arise of golden sun
  Incantations continue, spoken, almost done
A bolt of blinding light streaks out across the sky
  As the mage grins, "'Tis your last day for you will die."
Turning now to look down upon the packed courtyard

Great legions of armored men in iron wrought hard
Small darken clouds materialize overhead
80   Soon, any and all that stand before will be dead
Death and hatred unleashed to vanquish love and joy
Sending forth his army to conquer and destroy
The grey mage's black banners adorn long steel pikes
War horses covered in leather and sharpened spikes

Ferocious foot soldiers lightly armored for speed
The darkness is approaching for all to take heed

The Princess

A beautiful young princess barely through her teens
    Walking amongst her snow covered gardens, pristine
Inhaling the deep, crisp, clean, winter morning air
90   Flowing ribbons of violet and green from her hair
Wrapped against the cold within an emerald gown
    Gently draping her, from her shoulders and on down
Trees ladened with heavy snow bow down to the ground
    Whilst the pretty young princess spins and twirls all 'round
Falling down into the snow, the princess is laid
    Fanning out her arms, a snow angel is now made
Laughing and enjoying this beautiful cold day
    With an open heart, greeting all who come her way
Startled by a loud horn calling all men to arms
100   The princess rushes back to escape any harm
With her heart pounding, seeking her father, the king
    Whilst all of the four towers' bells begin to ring

"A vast black army marches from out of the west.
    You must make haste to castle east, for it is best."
To her, those would be her father's last words spoken
    For the peace she enjoyed is forever broken
To the stables she now goes with a quicken pace
    Mounts her golden mare, her heart continues to race
Embarking from the castle with two knights on hand
110   Adventuring forth to castle east across land
Riding hard and fast across the snow covered plains
    Princess holds on tightly to her golden mare's reins
Over hills, into the woods to escape her plight
    Darkness begins to fall to signal the cold night

The Young Man

A bolt of light explodes upon the brave knight's mail
    Young man leaps forth from brush catching knight without fail
Slowly and very gently down doth the knight go
    Laying the knight to rest softly into the snow
Young man kneels next to the knight upon bended knee
120   The mortal wounds of flowing blood are all he sees
This young man with heart and eager beyond his year
    With nothing much in this world to cause him great fear
Bowing close to the knight's head, feeling humbled, meek
    He must listen, for the knight is about to speak:

"Long ago, days still new
Taming lands so wild
Mother of hope so true
Bears forth a great child

Underneath blood red moon
Mother births second son
Dark shadow crosses moon
Heralding evil one

Two great sons are now born
One to dark, one to light
Balance cannot be torn
Burning sun, ever night

When darkness comes to call
Truth will free one and all

Evil being so shrew
A crystal heart styled
Into which evil flew
Light was now exiled

Dark brother would be soon
Consumed by what he'd done
Underneath blood red moon
His heart and crystal one

Destroys all with great scorn
Shadows cast, ever night
From the land life is torn
No more sun, only night

When darkness comes to call
Truth will free one and all

Great son knew what to do
Darkness could not run wild
Wrought from light a sword true
Hope for every child

Underneath night's new moon
Heart true to sword be one
For light will arrive soon
Truth pure, evil undone

Good again is now born
Once was dark is now light
Dark brother's crystal torn
Darkness lifted from night

For darkness cannot call
Truth has freed one and all"

Story once told, the quest is now revealed at last
    Burden lifted from knight to young man nobly passed
A living crystal filled with great evil was wrought
    Now to this peaceful land again evil is brought
"Take my sword and to your heart you must remain true.
130   For all of the world's hope, rests now upon just you."
Reaching for the sword, the knight hands over his blade
    Quest is passed by young man's oath, reluctantly made
Young man looks up to brilliant sun now high above
    His eyes falling upon this beautiful white dove

Gazing down upon the knight with tears in his eyes
    The brave knight smiles, breathes his last breath, and quickly dies
Grasping the sword tightly within his trembling hand
    Arising next to the knight he begins to stand
For now, he must find the knight's alabaster steed
140   To ride west, to complete this necessary deed

Black Army

Mage's black army marches across barren plains
 Destruction, devastation, over which they reign
Through fields of pure snow, soon to become only charred
 The horrors of battle leaving the land now marred
Thunderous sounds of hooves and boots marching as one
 Vast noir sea of death consumes all and everyone
The army falling upon a small peaceful town
 By the sword, villagers in their own blood will drown
Screams arise of terror and fear piercing through air
150 Mothers cry for their children, hearts filled with despair
Desperate men armed with makeshift weapons in hand
 Facing their fears with an heroic final stand
Some villagers gather what they can—try to flee
 A volley of arrows rains down—death sets them free
Blood thirsty black knights mounted upon armored steeds
 Charge forth into town unleashing horrific deeds
Upon these desperate men the black knights doth break
 Lifeless bodies in blood left behind in their wake

A mother holds her new born babe upon her breast
160 Knight takes his long sword, stabs through babe and mother's chest
Mother and babe's lifeless bodies to the ground laid
 No villager survives, not even those who strayed
Even in the church where people kneel and pray
 Knight's burst in, people scream, as they begin to slay
Young boy flees into the street, falls down with a thud
 As the ground turns into muddy rivers of blood
Every last man, woman, and child being dispatched
 Fiery torches are thrown upon roofs thatched
Death continues to march forward, no turning back

170   As smoke billows up, turning blue sky to black
    Mage looking through his crystal to behold this sight
        Grinning, "Soon the land will feel my dark deadly might."
    Mist begins to form within, slowly starts to swirl
        The images of death spiral around and twirl
Now the mist forms into the castle of the king
        Soon, the mage's army will come to make death sing
Evil is spreading out, darkness consuming all
        Across the land, death's shadow has begun to fall

Knight's Final Ride

Searching until the sun has fallen into night
180   The knight's alabaster steed is nowhere in sight
Young man decides to make camp and lights a fire
      A long journey awaits and he must now retire
Into sleep he doth fall, as he begins to dream
      Visions stir, premonitions to heed and redeem…
Blinding light shines from the sword true held upon high
      By a righteous white knight standing upon blue sky
Young man kneeling in fields of green with his arms raised
      Feeling completely humbled, awed, and somewhat dazed
White knight lowers the sword to young man's outstretched hands
190   *A new hero born to protect all of the lands*
Just as he is about to take the sword, he falls
      Light begins to fade, he screams, white knight heeds no call
The world is soon ripped and completely torn apart
      As young man plunges toward blood red crystal heart
His kind heart and soul are filled with nothing but fear . . .
      Startled awake by something licking at his ear

Jumping up and rubbing the sleep from weary eyes
      The dead knight's steed begins to materialize
Looking into the sad eyes of this noble horse
200   Young man soon realized what was his destined course
With a little struggle, picks up the knight in black
      Sets him upon the alabaster steed's strong back
Securing the knight in the saddle, best he can
      Noble knight upon steed soon parted from young man
Watching them ride slowly into day's dawning sun
      Knowing in his heart, the knight's story is now done

Drifting down from the morning's new sky from above
    Appears again, this same beautiful pure white dove
"A safe journey home to rest forever in peace."
210   Young man whispers as he pulls about him a fleece
To help guard himself against this unyielding cold
    Walking west, reluctant hero with heart of gold

Princess's Plight

Heading east through vast forest from the other side
    The princess with her two noble protectors ride
Galloping through the deep woods and cold winter's night
    Only with the stars and moon as their guiding light
With the day behind them and many more ahead
    Pair of knights remedied not the princess's dread
Her heart is burdened with the fears for her father
220   Prays for his safety to the eternal Mother
Her ordeal leaves her weary, worried, and so weak
    One of the knights fans out for shelter he must seek
Finding some refuge, the knight quickly hurries back
    Informs the princess of a small abandoned shack
Princess agrees and feels the cold bite under skin
    As a growing fear starts to fester deep within
Approaching this dark broken down little hovel
    Having an eerie feeling that doth not bode well
Cautiously approaching, the princess slowly walks
230   Upon reaching the threshold, suddenly she balks
A wolf starts to howl somewhere amongst the pines
    A cold shiver runs up and down princess's spine
Soon other wolves begin to take up the first's calls
    The knights hurry her through the open door; she falls
And upon a dirty floor the princess now lies
    Praying this horrid abode is not where she dies
The knights busily force the horses through the door
    As the princess quickly scrambles up from the floor
Knights draw their long swords—ready themselves to engage
240   Long steel swords slash into vicious wolves as they rage

Knights heroically hold hungry fierce wolves at bay
    To a darkened corner doth the scared princess stray
Fearful of losing all in the world she doth love
    Deep in the corner, she finds a little white dove
Mists begin to form and the darkness starts to fade
    Into a woman the small white dove is now made
Mother speaks softly, "Rest my child, you need not fear.
    Soon, all that is before will become very clear.
Head east to forest end, then west you must depart.
250   Find a man with the sword true and to his own heart."
Mother bends down, gives the princess a gentle kiss
    And princess is returned back to the black abyss
Of the hovel, as steel swords swing about and clang
    Against these ferocious wolves bearing deadly fangs
The brave knights continue in their gallant defense
    Unaware of the heavenly Mother's presence
Unrelenting, the fierce battle still rages on
    As the night gently drifts away towards the dawn
Bearing forth the day with its golden rays of sun
260   The last of the wolves depart, the battle now won
Burden of the siege done, from the defense now free
    Knights bow down on bended knee to Mother they see
Mother informs them all of their most urgent quest
    Of the man, sword, and the evil mage to the west
Princess and knights pledge to the Mother with their words
    Knights ask the Mother for a blessing on their swords
As fare-thee-wells are given, Mother points the course
    Princess and knights embark to discover hope's source
Their destiny awaits them, and they must not yield
270   With faith, hope, and truth as their unwavering shield
Surviving the attack of those horrible beasts
    Upon their horses, the three ride off to the east

The King

Behind walls of his great castle sits noble king
    Preparing himself against evil's undoing
Men quickly run back and forth with parchment in hand
    Informs of the black army's approach across land
King decrees his subjects to head for castle east
    Only the king's brave army will face this noir beast
The king will don his armor and fight aside knights
280   The king will not show his fear of this horrid plight
King summons his most trusted knight, beloved friend
    Asks him to lead if he comes to untimely end
The knight, king's loyal lord, with heavy heart agrees
    And with that, noble king makes his final decrees
Arising from throne with violet robes trimmed in gold
    King walks through his court; no other man is so bold
His crown never before carried such a great weight
    For the hour draws near, hoping it's not too late
Knights and nobles bow, as he walks across the floor
290   The king exits the great hall through the high arched door
Heading up marble stairs towards widow's tower
    Seeking some solace in this most dire hour
His thoughts stray to the memories of his late wife
    And how in death, she gave to him his daughter's life
Wonders now about the safety of the princess
    The daughter he loves and who tenderly doth miss
He ascends the staircase and spies the last room
    Opens the door, enters alone, ponders the doom
He looks down to his subject who gave him great love
300   As in through the window flies a tiny grey dove

In all of his many just and kind ruling years
    Has any moment brought upon him sorrowed tears
With hope's bright light dwindling within his tired heart
    This tiny grey dove starts to grow and break apart
Swarming 'cross the room, appears a murder of crows
    Attacking the king and out the window he goes
Through twilight abyss to his death broken king flies
    The crows vanish upon the ground where he now lies
In the vast forest, the princess feels her heart crack
310   Realizing her father has gone into black
Looking through his crystal heart, grins evil grey mage
    Soon, the rest of the land will feel his horrid rage…

Amidst The Chaos

. . . an interlude

. . . heavy darkened clouds spread out from mage's black keep
    No sun, stars, or moon nor hint of light doth now seep
Evil spreads out across this once peaceful good land
    From the terrible power within mage's hand
Pouring out from that blood red, evil crystal heart
    Destroying all in his path, ripping them apart
Villages that once were filled with laughter and joy
320   Upon them black army fell only to destroy
Word spreads out of noble king's untimely demise
    Beloved subjects carry on with tears in their eyes
Dead brave knight upon trusted steed to home doth ride
    So many good people have been cut down and died
Hope begins to dim and soon there is no more light
    Peaceful land now cast into the darkness of night
Princess with her two protectors ride to the east
    Having survived their battle with ferocious beasts
The young man continues his long walk to the west
330   The fate of the land, upon his shoulders doth rest
Across this troubled land covered in the cold snow
    Hope and faith dwindle and to the darkness doth go…

Encounter In The Forest

Through the frigid snow covered, vast sullen forest
    Princess and two knights ride east with so little rest
Heeding eternal Mother's words devotedly
    Searching for the young man true and determinedly
With unwavering guidance of tiny white dove
    Flying swiftly before them and slightly above
So many days and nights have gone into the past
340   They cometh upon a young man fleece wrapped at last
The white dove begins to circle above his head
    Reluctant hero to rescue the land from dread
"Pardon sir, my lady would like to have a word."
    One knight speaks, as princess is ready to be heard
Young man listens to princess's story, now told
    Feeling a tiny spark within his heart of gold
"I'm just a humble man with a life that is meek.
    You can have this sword, for glory I doth not seek."
Reluctant young man tries to plea, his words in vain
350   Princess dismounts, approaches with mare by her reins
"You sir, are the only one to wield the sword true.
    Our fate, and the land, depends on us, and you."
Young man thinks: *I'm not the man to be their hero*
    But by my oath made to that dead knight, I must go
The two knights converse and question the Mother's choice
    Neither one willing to divulge their doubts by voice
Openly to the young man or their young princess
    Hoping this is not folly leading to distress
Two savage hungry eyes watch eagerly this scene
360   From a safe distance where it could remain unseen
Readies itself to pounce forth and completely crush
    Upon companions, doth the silver dragon rush…

The Silver Dragon

With unnatural speed, like a flash of lightning
    Bearing sharp claws and ferocious fangs so frightening
Silver dragon attacks with a fierce blinding speed
    The dragon's hunger drives it to fulfill its need
A cold savage rage burns deeply within its eyes
    With a deep loud roar meant to shock and terrorize
Dragon attacks the two knights first with deadly claws
370   *Leaving the surprised knights to defend without pause*
Whilst dragon's powerful tail swings the other way
    Keeping reluctant hero and princess at bay
Dragon knocks away knights like leaves in a strong breeze
    One knight tries to rise up, but falls back on his knees
Fierce dragon now turns to young man and princess fair
    Disregarding the two knights without any care
Saliva drips from its fangs with such a great thirst
    Eyes them both deciding which to devour first
The dragon upon its legs rises up higher
380   *Looking down upon its prey, unleashes its fire*
Young man, with princess behind, raises the sword true
    Stands stoic in wrath's path thinking it's all he can do
A great energy flowed from within his gold heart
    Into the sword true and the dragon's flames doth part
Young man feeling like he is caught up in a dream
    Taking no notice to the princess as she screams
Young man lowers the sword and forward he doth charge
    Straight into the dragon's silver chest looming large
Piercing the dragon's heart, slaying this silver beast
390   *For now, the victory is his on which to feast . . .*

Gazing upon dragon's body, young man turns 'round
 His eyes rest upon the princess on unscorched ground
Moving towards her, with open hand, he doth greet
 Helping the princess arise and stand on her feet
Together they move to check her protectors' plight
 Discovering them just dazed, these two valiant knights
Assisting them upon their feet, doth knights arise
 Looking upon young man with respect in their eyes
The knights honor the young man and give him their hand
400 Hero of light is now born to release this land
From the grey mage and evil crystal that was wrought
 With young man and sword true, to the land, hope is brought

Night Has Fallen

Evil grey mage schemes within his sullen noir keep
    Devious ire flows through his soul very deep
Watching through the blood red crystal within his hand
    Destruction and death pour across once peaceful land
Darken clouds so thick block out the sun overhead
    Transforms this great land into dark world of the dead
Reveling in the evil might of his power
410   Plunging the people into the midnight hour
Grey mage plots his next move to take and overthrow
    King's castle and all his remaining noble foes
With lordly contempt, walks into his onyx hall
    Summons one of his acolytes at beckon call
Demands some roast mutton and a goblet of mead
    And to summon the sorceress for a dark deed
Sitting at a long wooden table made from oak
    Taking satisfaction with his plan's master stroke
Enters into the hall with flowing hair of jet
420   Struts the sorceress in a crimson silhouette...

Enter Sorceress

She thinks . . .

. . . "with all that power you are only a great fool
    For you think of me as your obedient tool
For I know the secret of that red crystal heart
    And from this world, evil mage, you will soon depart
That crystal will consume and devour your sad soul

In order to make itself once again now whole
You think that you are in control of its power
But you will soon know in that final dark hour
Soon that crystal will make you mad and you will fall
430 *I will come in and answer your final death's call."*

She stands with obedient daggers in her eyes
  Concealing her evil deep within where it lies
"The sword true is hidden from my all seeing eye.
  Go east and find it then bring it to me or die."
Mage commands her with a deep fiery cold voice
  Leaving her no options or any other choice
"This task will be done as you command, my dark lord,"
  Replies the sorceress in the same evil chord
Bowing to the grey mage, ready to take her leave
440 For in the end (for the mage) she will never grieve
She then turns and walks out through the onyx hall's door
  As mage gazes 'pon crystal to savor his war
Images stir to show the castle of the king
  His black army approaches to make the doom ring

Battle At King's Castle

Golden amber sun slowly rises in the east
>From the west approaches mage's horrid noir beast
Darken clouds form and begin to move overhead
Heralding the coming of such an evil dread
Days and nights, many villages razed, now to siege
450   This mighty great castle without its noble liege
Black army's destruction across this peaceful land
Has brought them to king's castle at which they now stand
King's loyal lord remaining true to his sworn word
Shouting his commands; sounds of war is all that's heard
Black army forms up ranks with a savage blood lust
With a mighty roar, upon king's castle they thrust
Rushing forth to the moat and mighty castle walls
Through this wave, many of the black army doth fall
Upon battlements, crossbows 'lease their deadly bolts
460   Whilst catapults hurl massive stones with mighty jolts
Black knights answer back with fiery arrows and spears
With unrelenting volleys to instill great fear
Over the high walls the fiery arrows doth go
Noble defenders scramble as the flames doth grow
Screams arise from men as they die, pierce through the air
For in war, there is only death and great despair
Many men on both sides are cut down and soon die
Underneath the darkened, heavy cloud covered sky
The fierce battle continues to rage, life is torn
470   From day to night, dawn to dusk, and back to the morn

Journey West

After a very brief, but a much needed rest
    The four companions of good journey to the west
The princess, two noble knights, and hero of light
    Continue to ride on towards evil's black night
Through the vast forest gripped by the winter's harsh cold
    To end the evil grey mage's sinister hold
Upon this once peaceful and beautiful great land
    With the sword true in the reluctant hero's hand
Under protection, guidance of Mother above
480   Flying above them as a little, pure white dove
Companions cometh upon a lonely old man
    Old man tells them of the noble king's final plan
And how the great king fell to his untimely death
    Old man stops his tale to catch his quivering breath
His face strained, gaunt, and drained of blood, appearing pale
    Catching his breath continues on with his sad tale
With disbelief and anger they listen in shock
    As the sad, tired old man continues to talk
All of the king's subjects journey to castle east
490   Leaving the king's lord and knights to face mage's beast
The young princess saddened by this, begins to cry
    As cold white snow starts to fall from the cloud filled sky
Princess and young man dismount from her golden mare
    Walking together to the old man, truly care
Young man and princess offer a hand and some food
    Young man's spark within his golden heart is renewed
As princess comforts old man with gentle caress
    Young man wants to lift that burden of pain and stress
From 'pon her that has been placed, a tremendous strife

500   A cruel evil twist of fate to her regal life
Princess turns to her knights, makes a royal decree
    "Assist this old man and find my people that flee.
Then to castle east, ask for help against this mage
    For this great evil cannot continue to rage.
With the sword true, we will go west to evil's source
    For Mother and fate have shown us our destined course."
Noble knights agree and nod their helmeted heads
    For hope glimmers through this darkness and evil dread

Fall Of King's Castle

As the seventh sun rises to break the new dawn
510   The fierce battle at king's castle still rages on
Noble defenders high upon the castle walls
     The black army in the field, still willing to brawl
Putrid foul stench of death fills the morning air
     As the black army forms up to the horns that blare
Brave knights wake and rush to defend with all their might
     Against this continuing force of hate and fright
Bracing themselves at the gate for another rush
     The black army charges forward only to crush
The mighty king's castle and all that stand inside
520   Across the battlefield flows this evil's noir tide
Over the body-filled moat upon the closed gate
     The black army's ram doth slam to end this stalemate
The sturdy wooden timbers crack, break, then give way
     For the brave noble defenders 'tis their last day
Into the king's castle doth the black army barge
     The noble defenders rally to face their charge
As sharp swords clash upon shields and sounds of steel ring
     Horrid screams of men arise as death starts to sing
Black army tramples over the fallen and dead
530   As castles stones are covered with blood flowing red
King's loyal lord makes for one last desperate stand
     The battle is lost as sword falls from his dead hand
Grey mage gazing in the crystal sees victory
     Whilst grinning at the destruction that he doth see
Black army victorious at a heavy cost
     Into the cold, dark night, amber sun is now lost

Friend Or Foe

Many cold days and nights now gone without much rest
    As hero and princess continue to ride west
The hope of the land now rests upon the sword true
540   And the companions of light, now down to just two
Riding upon the back of this swift golden mare
    The two companions with gold hearts deeply doth care
For the terrible plight of this once peaceful land
    And for each other, to face evil hand in hand
Out of the forest, over hills, across vast plains
    Companions of light ride to stop grey mage's reign
Of destruction, evil terror, and horrid fright
    As the golden sun rises to lift the dark night
Upon the path a curious sight to behold
550   A scarlet robed woman standing silent and bold
With long flowing hair of jet draping down her back
    The companions of light and hope stop in their tracks
Young man dismounts, cautiously forward to parley
    With the crimson woman to hear what she would say

As the princess watches the two figures confer
    A strange uneasiness begins to build and stir
The conversation ends, the two begin to walk
    Towards princess, doubtful young man returns to talk
With the woman in crimson and long hair of jet
560   Following him behind and offering no threat
About the evil mage at his sinister keep
    As mistrust blooms into princess's heart doth creep
Silently, scarlet sorceress watches closely
    As two noble companions discuss secretly

What to do with this woman in a robe of red
    And the utter evil of the grey mage's dread
Within her mind, the scheming sorceress doth plot
    To her advantage and to good companions not
Discussion complete, a fragile alliance formed
570   A dangerous pact with evil has just been born
To the day's darkening cloud filled skies high above
    Flies off Mother as this beautiful pure white dove
For her part in this tale is now over and done
    As the three continue west to the setting sun…

Before The Fall

. . . an interlude

. . . darkness consumes all of the cold, snow covered land
    As evil still pours forth from the grey mage's hand
The dark cloud filled skies hide the brilliant golden sun
    As now the day and cold black night have become one
No more doth birds' beautiful songs fill morning's air
580   This once peaceful land plunged deep into great despair
Death's final dark shadow to all has come calling
    The mighty king's castle has finally fallen
King's subjects flee through the forest to castle east
    Trying to escape the mage's evil noir beast
With the guidance of two devoted noble knights
    To seek some help and safety from this horrid plight
Princess, hero, and sorceress onward they ride
    To the west to stop the grey mage's evil pride
As the sorceress hatches her sinister scheme
590   Bringing to life the young hero's earlier dream
Black army is victorious at heavy cost
    As hope has faded to the dark and is now lost
Night has cometh to stay with no hope of day's dawn
    Black army turns east unleashing its deadly storm…

Ambush

A few days of rest for mage's army of black
  Marching east for another castle to attack
Slowly trudging through snow covered land they move on
  Cloaked in darkness, no more brilliant light of day's dawn
For heavy bleak clouds blanket the once bright blue sky
600 Shielding the heavens from the people 'bout to die
This powerful horrid evil is on the loose
  Once peaceful great land is caught fast within its noose
Deep into the forest the black army doth go
  Ominous clouds unleash lightning and heavy snow
Caught up in nature's relentless winter's cold blast
  The mage's black army is forced to stop at last.

. . .

Meanwhile across the land and far off to the west
  Hero, princess, and sorceress ride without rest
Deep into the evil grey mage's bleak dark realm
610 As feelings of despair begin to overwhelm
Cautiously approaching the grey mage's noir keep
  Uncertainty into princess's heart doth creep
Silent as the dead of night, no guards at their post
  Eerie whispers of wind and the keep's evil ghosts
Outside the grey walls, the three dismount in the snow
  Walking slowly into the castle—three doth go
Sinister sorceress leads them to the courtyard
  No signs of any life, no animals, no guards
The trap is set, the time ticks on slowly and nears

620 Suddenly, sorceress turns, smiles, then disappears
Too late, hero and princess doth soon realize
  As the armed guards begin to materialize
And soon the two brave companions are quickly caught
  Bound fast, and to the grey mage as trophies be brought
The noble companions of light now have been crossed
  The quest for peace cast into darkness ever lost.

. . .

Back as the storm rages amidst the forest trees
  The black army tries to move forward to get free
Of this, nature's wrath, winter's unforgiving plight
630 Struggling to survive with all their strength and might
Many men under this storm have died and fallen
  As thunderous drums start to beat death knell's calling
From somewhere off into this deep forest's distance
  Battling the elements with much resistance
As black army prepares for an epic battle
  Trees start to come to life, as the branches rattle
King's subjects with brave, noble knights from castle east
  Have come to stand against evil mage's noir beast
This is the final, noble, desperate last stand
640 The last glimmer of hope for this once peaceful land

The Final Battle

Hero and young princess with their hands bound in rope
    Escorted by armed guards have lost faith and all hope
Through darkened passageways the prisoners are led
    Both pondering their fate, being consumed by dread
All are stopped by the sorceress with hair of jet
    Standing before them in a crimson silhouette
Approaching the guards, silently, without a word
    Slowly reaches her hand out and takes the true sword
"Leave us now. I will take these usurpers with me."
650   Leering at the prisoners, "You won't try to flee?"
Within the princess anger ignites by this spark
    Ire and rage building within this noble monarch
Lunging at diabolic sorceress, she flies
    "You doth frighten me not." Defiance in her eyes
Hero rushes forward quickly to intercede
    For caution, two companions of light must now heed
Scarlet sorceress eerily laughing out loud
    Princess standing firm holding her regal head proud
"Fear not you two, for this is all going to plan;
660   The only way to get close to that evil man."
With that said, sorceress loosens the ropes that bind
    Plotting her next move within her dark scheming mind
Thinking *"these two are now my noble little tools*
    Oh my vile blind mage, now who is the jester's fool."
The princess's heart and mind are full of mistrust
    Patiently and silently she watches, she must
As the sorceress gives them the final details
    Princess and hero must be strong or they will fail
Away the two are led to the bleak onyx hall

670 Where at last, grey mage's evil now comes to call
Far off in the distance, a bell begins to ring
  Sounds of steel swords clash about and begin to sing.

. . .

Deep within the vast forest with snow covered trees
  Army of knights with loyal subjects that are free
Stoically stand against mage's evil noir beast
  To prevent this evil from reaching castle east
Led by the princess's two devoted brave knights
680 Goodness and truth cometh together, stand and fight
Mage's army of black, confused, battered, weakened
  Scrambles to meet their foe—fight to the bitter end
Just as the horrific storm breaks from darkened sky
  Golden rays of light shine upon the men from high
Into the bubbling noir sea, free knights doth charge
  Straight to the black army's heart they boldly barge
Whilst the sharp steel swords swing about, slash, clash, and ring
  King's free subjects attack with clubs as freedom sings
Many are cut down into the new fallen snow
690 As their blood is spilled and soon to death they doth go
Staining the snow with their blood flowing ruby red
  Brave men, free men, mage's men litter the ground—dead
Amongst the forest trees, the battle rages on
  Under the golden sun of the day's reborn dawn
Righteous men battling for freedom at all cost
  For hope returns, carries on, and all is not lost
The black army is beaten and soon driven back
  Under the heroic people's gallant attack
In the heavens above shines a bright golden sun
700 For this battle is over and light has now won
But for the companions of light far to the west
  Their strength and conviction will be put to the test.

. . .

Princess and hero stand before grey mage at last
>	Into darkness, noble companions are now cast
The doom has arrived to this once peaceful great land
>	Towards mage sorceress struts with true sword in hand
Vile grey mage laughing, "You thought you could defeat me."
>	Defiant hero replies, "Free me! We will see."
Fierce fire burns deeply within both men's eager eyes
710	One will triumph—stand over his foe as he dies
Princess watches the scene as it slowly unfolds
>	Gathering within her strength to stand very bold
Silence falls as the tension fills the onyx hall
>	A flash of light and to the ground doth hero fall
Mage drunk on his power towards hero he walks
>	The sorceress, behind the mage, now slowly stalks
Hero writhing in extreme agony and pain
>	Princess quickly rushes forward only in vain
Mage twitches his hand, princess flies into the door
720	Slams hard and falls limp upon the cold, black stone floor
Mage stands gloating over his fallen noble foe
>	Unaware of sorceress, as she slyly throws
The sword true to the struggling hero of light
>	Blinding light explodes as hero rises in might
Grey mage blinded, stumbles as he tries to leap back
>	Now sorceress, from behind, begins her attack
Hero rushes to check 'pon the fallen monarch
>	Princess rises slowly, notices flashing sparks
Mage, sorceress locked within an epic battle
730	As the keep's stone walls shake and begin to rattle
A crucial blow and sorceress is knocked aside
>	Towards the companions, vengeful grey mage now strides
The young princess with fear in her eyes yells, "Look out!"
>	Hero turns around ready for the final bout
'Pon the floor, sorceress clutches the crystal heart
>	Switch made sleathfully upon her sinister part

Young princess throws herself quickly into harm's path
     Saving the hero from grey mage's evil wrath
Brilliant light starts to radiate from the sword true
740   As brave hero lunges and swiftly runs sword through
The diabolic evil mage in robes of grey
     Ending the dark night's reign over the light of day
Hero rushes to fallen princess with great love
     As through a brightened window flies a lone white dove
Dove transforms into the great eternal Mother
     As sorceress leaves under confusion's cover
Brave hero embraces princess in joy and bliss
     Princess rejoices at the touch of his soft kiss
Mother speaks, "Evil defeated here in the west.
750   Return to your home east, you both deserve to rest."
For this part of the tale is now over and done
     As good has triumphed over great evil and won

Happily Ever After...?

Snow melted, heralding the arrival of spring
    As the wedding bells at king's castle start to ring
Brave hero and young princess are soon to be wed
    And rebuild the kingdom from the grey mage's dread
The royal subjects gather in the vast courtyard
    Covered with red and white roses, no longer marred
From the destruction of this winter's cold dark past
760   A new peace comes to this land that will grow and last
Battlefields no longer charred or covered in blood
    No more are paths flowing rivers of crimson mud
Villagers, no more in terror, need to run—flee
    Under evil's destructive force, they are now free
The farmers toil in their fields, now becoming green
    The land is full of peace, love, happiness—serene
For light has triumphed over the dark that was wrought
    From evil crystal heart and good is again brought
To the kingdom across all of its great vast land
770   As hero and princess rule in love, hand in hand
This great land no longer suffers in evil's pain
    Under light's righteous, true, prosperous, loving reign
Alas, far to the south, evil begins to scheme
    To shatter peace's wonderful, joyous, great dream
As the sinister sorceress with hair of jet
    Plots her move to once again make the kingdom fret
From the great evil power of the crystal heart
    And destroy the land; to rip happiness apart
To bring darkness and death, hope and dreams she must slay
780   But that's a tale to be told for another day.

www.ingramcontent.com/pod-product-compliance
Lightning Source LLC
Chambersburg PA
CBHW031545060726
47590CB00004BA/1523